SPIRIT QUEST

SPIRIT QUEST

Diane Silvey
Illustrated by Joe Silvey

BEACH HOLME PUBLISHING

VANCOUVER

This edition published by Beach Holme Publishing, #226–2040 West 12th Avenue, Vancouver, BC, V6J 2G2, with the assistance of The Canada Council and the BC Ministry of Small Business, Tourism and Culture. This is a Sandcastle Book. Teacher's guide available from Beach Holme by calling 1-888-551-6655.

This is a work of fiction. Names, characters, places, and incidents are the product of the author's imagination or are used fictitiously, and any resemblance to actual persons, living or dead, events or locales is entirely coincidental.

Edited by Antonia Banyard and Joy Gugeler
Cover illustration by Joe Silvey
Cover design by Barbara Munzar
Type design by Carolyn Stewart
Photo credit (Diane Silvey): Dorothy Haggeart
Photo credit (Joe Silvey): Alana Herman

CANADIAN CATALOGUING IN PUBLICATION DATA:

Silvey, Diane
    Spirit quest
(a sandcastle book)
Illustrations by Joe Silvey.
ISBN 0-88878-376-0
I. Coast Salish Indians - Fiction. I. Silvey, Joe
II. Title. III. Series
PS8587.I278S65 1997C813'.54C96-901059-1
PR9199.3.S51767S65 1997

For Angela, Joe, Carol, Jason and Max

Grandfather laid his hands gently on Kaya's and Tala's shoulders. He counselled the twins softly, "The path ahead is treacherous, you must head north toward the mountains. Listen to your heart, it will guide you to the stolen box. The box holds all the sacred qualities our people cherish: love, kindness, truth, honesty, gentleness and generosity. Unless you return the box to our village, our people will become mean and small of heart." The twins made a pact then that if one of them got lost or hurt, the other would carry on to complete the important mission.

"We will not fail your trust Grandfather," Kaya and Tala pledged.

"I cannot go with you, for the trip ahead is too arduous for an old man, but my spirit will be with you," Grandfather assured them.

❖❖❖

Tala and Kaya started on their journey just before daybreak. They carried only a small sack each, because they knew they must travel quickly. If their mission failed, their people would be condemned to unhappiness for eternity. They crossed the high ridge to the east and left behind all that was safe and familiar.

Tala and Kaya continued over the ridge and headed down into the valley. This valley was deeper and darker than their own. There were no birds singing in the trees. The ground was strewn with moss and branches. Little sunlight filtered through the thick foliage. They followed the path that twisted into the forest, losing sight of the mountains to the north.

Parts of the trail were overgrown with salal-berry bushes and caused them to lose sight of the route. They found it again only to lose it once more on a rocky bank. As they had been traveling for several hours, they grew tired and frustrated. Finally they came to a clearing, but the mountain ridge was nowhere to be seen.

To the right of them was a meadow overgrown with straggly weeds, stretching as far as the eye could see. To the left was a dark and somber cedar forest. The path that they had lost was now clearly visible, leading into the woods. They followed it as the light grew dimmer and dimmer. Rotting wood and decaying branches lay on each side of the path.

A sharp scraping noise to one side made them stop dead in their tracks. They stood frozen, unsure whether to run or to remain where they were. Their breathing resounded against the tree trunks.

They heard the noise again and whirled around to see two dead trees rubbing together in the wind. They relaxed, daring to breathe deeply once more. Tala laughed nervously.

They walked deeper into the forest, whistling loudly to reassure themselves. The trees were so thick they blocked the last rays of sunlight. Dusk was falling quickly and the twins could barely see the path.

"Should we go on or camp for the night?" Tala asked.

"It is getting very dark but each minute we delay the box is being taken farther and farther away," Kaya said.

They both decided to carry on, putting one foot in front of the other, gingerly groping their way along in the dark. Suddenly they came to a clearing where a large shape shimmered in the dim light. In the middle of the clearing was a massive cedar tree trunk, at least four metres in diameter.

The path led around to the right and left of the trunk. Kaya motioned to Tala to scout around the tree to the left side and he would go to the right.

Kaya crept around the tree with her spear held tightly in hand. She came to a fire pit and felt the ashes; they were cold.

Tala inched around the base of the tree but stopped when he heard rustling noises in the brush. He thought it was Kaya and grinned. He had made it around the tree first. He tiptoed around the corner to tease her and a startled grouse flew out of the brush in front of him. Tala yelled and dropped to his knees, grasping his spear. Kaya, hearing her brother yell, leapt up from the fire pit and rushed toward him.

"It's all right, I was just startled by a grouse. Did you find anything?" Tala said.

"I found a fire pit but it looks like it hasn't been used recently," replied Kaya.

They decided to spend the night and gathered wood for their fire. Once they had the fire going, they made plans for the next morning. They ate some of the dried fish that grandfather had packed.

The fire made loud crackling noises in the silent forest. The light from the flames illuminated the shadows of the moving branches whose darkened limbs seemed to stretch into the night. Exhausted, they both fell asleep with their spears in their hands. They slept unaware of the eyes in the forest watching them.

2

Kaya awoke in the morning cold and hungry. When she rolled over she discovered her brother was no longer beside her. She leapt to her feet, shouting his name. In her haste she didn't see the arrow he had drawn in the dirt. Kaya ran around the tree and found fresh footprints. She thought the footprints were Tala's and decided to follow them. They headed into a ravine. There were also footprints in the mud by the riverbank. Some of the footprints were too big and could not possibly belong to Tala.

Tala must have been taken by kidnappers! She ran up the slope as quickly as she could reaching the top of the hill in time to see figures in the distance going over the ridge. With fear in her heart, she broke into a run.

❖ ❖ ❖

Tala had awakened before his sister and decided to find a high vantage point to look for the mountains to the north. In case Kaya woke before he came back, he had drawn an arrow in the dirt in the direction he had gone. When he returned to the deserted clearing, he became alarmed and set out in search for her. Tala found several sets of footprints and realized that the smaller tracks were his sister's. Were the other tracks from the evil ones who had stolen his people's sacred box? He sprinted off, determined to come to Kaya's rescue.

Kaya was gaining ground on the evil ones, whom she believed had taken her brother. To avoid being discovered, she followed at a distance. The element of surprise was her only ally. Kaya marched when the evil ones marched and rested when they rested. They headed up a steep hill and over the crest. She stayed behind on the other side to listen for voices.

After a few moments, she went to the top of the hill to see if she could spot Tala. This must be their camp. She heard a loud snap as a branch broke. Kaya's heart raced and she dared not breathe. Had the evil ones spotted her? She saw a figure out of the corner of her eye and dropped to the ground where she lay, frozen. The footsteps came nearer and nearer. Through the bushes in front of her she could see the boots of a guard.

What was that deafening noise in her ears? Was it only the pounding of her own heart? She felt as if it would burst and she tightened her fingers around her spear in a death grip.

Tala kept losing the trail of small footprints; each time it took precious minutes to find them again. He was so intent on following them he did not see what awaited ahead.

Suddenly his senses detected the familiar and terrifying scent of wolverine. Long ago, Grandfather had killed one of these animals when it had come into the village. Until he had, no one had felt safe. The people believed that the devil himself inhabited the body of the wolverine. The animal's fetid breath permeated the air.

Tala whirled around. The animal's jaws dripped with saliva and low growling noises came from deep within its throat. The animal's razor sharp claws swiped at Tala with lightening speed. Tala ducked but lost his footing and went sliding down the bank onto a small ledge. The wolverine leapt, barely missing Tala and raised his paw in attack.

Tala had trained all his young life to become a great hunter but nothing could have prepared him for the overpowering fear he felt now. He held onto his spear for dear life.

The wolverine raised his paw to strike again, when all of a sudden something swooped in front of the animal's face. The wolverine slashed at it, lost his balance and started to slide down the bank towards Tala.

Tala felt the adrenaline coursing through his body. He positioned himself and threw the spear with all his strength into the wolverine's eye. Frenzied, the wolverine thrashed around, howling like the devil. Tala was trapped on the ledge with the wounded wolverine sliding towards him.

If he jumped, the fall to the rocks below would surely kill him. Tala stood his ground, knowing that he could never get up the bank past the wolverine. He prepared to die a proud hunter.

3

A pair of wings fluttered in front of Tala's eyes as an eagle swooped down in the direction of the wolverine, now blinded and in pain. He reared up and swiped at the eagle. The wolverine lost his footing, and when pieces of the bank started to give way the animal stumbled and plunged over the edge of the cliff, falling to the jagged rocks below. Tala collapsed to his knees, exhausted. He heard laughter and looked around just as the eagle landed beside him. A small creature, a gnome-like boy, rode on the eagle's back. He jumped off and ran toward Tala.

Laughing, the boy said, "My name is Yaket, but people call me Y. What's your name? What's the matter? Frog got your tongue? You're not scared are you?"

Tala replied, "No, of course not. My name is Tala."

"Where are you going? Are you alone? Do you have anything sweet to eat?" Y said.

Tala laughed and said, "You have so many questions! Do you ever slow down?"

Y stuttered, "What do you mean slow down? Are you implying that my talking, talking is too fast, fast? Maybe you just listen too slowly!" he said, turning his back on Tala.

"I didn't mean to hurt your feelings," Tala said.

Y whirled around with a grin. "That's OK. Everybody says I talk too much. But I ask you, if you don't talk, how are you going to learn? Which way are you going? North? South? East? West?"

Tala said he was headed north on an important mission, but his sister has been kidnapped by the evil ones and he must rescue her. "I was following the path but lost it just before I met the wolverine," Tala said.

Y gave a short whistle and the eagle came over. Y jumped on the eagle's back, looked at Tala and said, "Well, come on, climb on, time's a-wasting, whatcha waiting for? Not scared . . . ."

"No, I'm not scared," Tala quickly cut in.

The eagle soared into the air. They were soon above the trees and staring at the mountain range to the north. He was torn: should he head north to complete his mission and rescue his people or listen to his heart and find his sister? Kaya and Tala had made a pact to let nothing stand in the way of completing the mission. He knew he must rescue the village but his sister could be in danger.

Y said, "Which way?"

Tala replied, "North," knowing that he couldn't break his promise.

The eagle veered to the north, his mighty wings fanning the air which whooshed against Tala's face. He felt elated but at the same time slightly uneasy.

The eagle landed at the base of the mountain. Y said, "I will search for your sister, you continue on your journey," and with that he abruptly flew off.

Tala headed up the mountain until he came to the pass that Grandfather had described to him. He went over it and came to a cliff jutting out from the mountain. Grandfather had told him to follow his heart. He climbed up on the rocky ledge and faced the east.

He took the leather pouch out of his sack and opened it. The bundle held Grandfather's medicine and a quartz crystal. He carefully pulled out the quartz and laid it on a slab of slate. He gathered three sticks the same length, size and texture. He tied them together into a pyramid and carefully placed the crystal on top of the sticks.

He crossed his legs and sat facing the crystal as the last light faded from the sky. He must not let his mind wander, lest he be possessed by the evil ones whose eerie voices called to him, "Tala, Tala, come to us. We will show you the box. Follow us, Tala. Remember the village, Tala."

With a sense of urgency in their voices they tried harder to tempt him. They held out their arms offering

Tala a magnificent bow and arrow to distract him from his quest. "Your people need help Tala — quickly, hurry. We only want to help. Trust us Tala, trust us."

Tala remembered his grandfather's words, "Think only pure thoughts, keep your mind and heart pure." Tala was tempted many times throughout the night but he resisted. He was exhausted by the time the first rays of light lit up the sky and struck the crystal. It glowed radiantly and formed a triangle of light, framing an island directly off shore. Tala knew then where to find the treasured box.

Kaya lay on the ground afraid to breathe. The guard passed and she was safe for the moment. She had to find somewhere nearby to hide so she could watch the camp and find where her brother was being held captive.

Creeping through the wet salal bushes, Kaya came to the mouth of a cave. Strange carvings decorated its entrance. She looked at the double-headed sea serpent carved in stone above her head. She listened, but could hear no sound from inside the cave. She went in thinking it would provide protection from the cold night air.

The arch slowly shifted as the grey stone changed into scales and the serpents noiselessly slithered to the ground, following her into the cave. The serpents knew they would dine well tonight.

Kaya could hardly see in the dark. She wondered if she should turn back or camp for the night. She

felt something on her face. Could it be the wind? Perhaps she was close to an exit. She decided to press on. Yes, it was getting lighter, and as she walked, the tunnel began to widen. Suddenly, she came into a large room in which the ceiling and floor were covered with stalagmites and stalactites.

Kaya heard a noise back in the tunnel and thought she could just make out a shape moving in the dark. Then she realized there were two shapes slithering towards her. Serpents! Two enormous serpents! She spun around and ran across the open chamber.

In front of her were two tunnels, one leading up and the other down. She quickly chose the one which led upwards, and came to an opening which faced a sheer cliff impossible to climb or, her other alternative, to descend. There was a straight drop to the cliff's base.

She was trapped! If she went back down the tunnel, the serpents would kill her, but Kaya knew she had to risk it. The serpents moved slowly – perhaps she could make it.

She raced down the tunnel as fast as her legs would fly and came to the open chamber where one of the serpents lay coiled and ready to strike. With her heart in her mouth Kaya plunged into the tunnel leading downwards. The serpent struck, missing Kaya's head by centimetres. Kaya continued down the tunnel and came out into the daylight. She looked for an escape, but she was at a dead end. Again, she faced the steep cliffs. She had no way out except to climb.

Kaya looked desperately for any crevice or niche she could dig her fingers into and pull herself up, feeling with her feet at the same time for any toehold. Kaya had climbed hundreds of cliffs with Tala and was very nimble. But when she was halfway up the cliff she realized she could go no further.

The rock was sheer and smooth with only a tiny shrub growing out of the cliff. When she reached for it, it loosened, setting Kaya off balance. Her feet slipped and she struggled down the cliff making a desperate lunge at another bush close by. Pebbles and rocks clattered into the ravine. Kaya's muscles ached and her arms shook as she pulled herself to temporary safety.

The serpents waiting directly below were pummelled with pebbles and rocks. They hissed loudly.

She started to climb and, just as she scrambled onto the top of the cliff, a dark shadow appeared on the ground in front of her.

Kaya whirled around with her knife in hand. She was ready to face whatever evil was to befall her next. She could only make out a dark shape coming straight toward her and ducked beneath its wings. Grasping the hilt of her knife she spun around, ready for it to attack.

Kaya looked in amazement as a huge eagle landed

in front of her. Riding on the eagle's back was a small boy.

Kaya called out, "Greetings, Little One."

"Who are you calling little?" Yaket replied.

Kaya laughed and said, "No offence meant."

"You sure look like your brother," Y said.

"My brother?" Kaya said, startled.

"Yes, Tala and I fought a fierce wolverine. Actually there were two wolverines, I killed both of them and rescued Tala."

"Where is Tala?" Kaya asked sharply.

"Did you know your brother is looking for you?" Y said.

"Where is he?" Kaya yelled.

"Off searching for some silly old box," Y answered.

Kaya was so frustrated she picked Y up and shook him shouting, "Where is my brother?" A loud clap of thunder rumbled across the sky. Kaya put Y down and looked around. Y said, "Oh! Oh! Now you've done it!"

"Done what?"Kaya asked.

"Made Father angry, that's what!" Y replied.

Kaya could feel a strong wind around her ankles which grew stronger and stronger until Kaya's and Y's body were enclosed in a vortex that spun faster and faster as it lifted them into the air. Kaya screamed as her feet left the ground.

The funnel of air pulled them steadily upward until it stopped abruptly, depositing them on a cloud. Kaya looked down at her feet in amazement. She was standing on a white cloud and staring out at other clouds in a sea of incredible blue sky.

Kaya turned around, looking for Y. Her eyes widened as she looked up and up at the frame of an enormous longhouse decorated with a design of two killer whales. In the middle of the longhouse stood a tall pole and at its base, the mouth of a huge bird served as an entrance. The house posts on each end of the longhouse would take four grown men holding hands to span them. Even more amazing, the longhouse did not rest on the clouds but hung suspended in air.

A booming voice rang out and Kaya turned, astonished to see the God of Thunder. He was taller than anyone Kaya had ever seen before, his body radiating with a luminous light. His handsome face appeared stern. "What have you been doing now Y?" he asked.

Y answered, "Nothing, Father."

"Then why was Kaya shaking you?"

Kaya asked, "How do you know my name?"

"I know all my people's names," he answered. "Why were you shaking my son?"

Kaya said, "My brother is in great danger and I need to find him quickly. Y knows where he is but he wouldn't stop talking long enough to answer my questions." She paused then asked, "Can you please help me find my brother?"

The God of Thunder replied, "No I must not interfere in the destiny of mortals. I will let Y lead you to the Medicine Man. He is a wise man and sees many things which can help you."

Kaya and Y walked towards the Medicine Man's house as Y muttered to himself, "It's just not right, why am I always in trouble? I ask you. I never do anything wrong. But oh no, I always get blamed." Y kicked a clump of clouds and sent them flying in all directions.

Kaya let out a loud scream – she was falling through the clouds! Her feet dangled in the air and she desperately lunged forward trying to hoist herself back up with the help of Y who grabbed her hand and pulled with all his might. Kaya came hurtling up sending Y tumbling over backwards.

Y looked very indignant and said, "Feel with your feet when you walk and make sure the cloud is solid. There are lots of air pockets up here!"

They came to a longhouse smaller than the one they were in earlier. The sign for good and evil, the double headed sea serpent, faced inward. Between the two snakes was a ring of fire. A man sat hunched over at the back of the longhouse. There was a huge fire in the pit and smoke curled upward through the open boards in the ceiling. The smoky atmosphere made the shaman appear frightening and mystical.

Y spoke to the shaman in a trembling voice, "Medicine Man, I ask that you receive us."

A powerful resonant voice from the shadows asked, "What business do you come on?"

"My friend Kaya has lost her brother and requires your assistance, Medicine Man," Y said.

"Are my great powers to be used for one who cannot even speak for herself?" the Medicine Man answered.

Kaya spoke up saying, "I am searching for my brother." The fire flared up, sending sparks shooting everywhere.

"You must not speak to the shaman so, he has a title," Y whispered.

Kaya understood and quickly said, "Great Medicine Man, I ask that you help me locate my brother."

The shaman shook his rattle in a sharp steady

rhythm, raising his hands above his head. He started to chant and as he did so the flames parted to reveal the image of Tala sitting on the ledge of a cliff. Kaya cried out when she saw Tala in the dark surrounded by evil spirits.

The shaman said, "He is in no danger as long as he keeps pure thoughts in his mind. He must pass this test."

"We must go quickly and help him," Y said to Kaya.

"No, he must undertake this quest alone," Kaya answered.

"He will not be finished until he finds his protective spirit. It will appear to him in the form of an animal. We must wait until daybreak."

Kaya and Y climbed on the eagle and headed toward a mountain near the one on which Tala was perched. They slept uneasily, anxiously awaiting daylight. Kaya would undergo her own ritual soon but this night was Tala's alone. Kaya's thoughts were with her twin and she willed him strength.

6

As the long night faded and morning came, Tala awoke tired and weak. He stretched and moved his cramped body as he looked up and saw a sudden movement in the clouds. He stared, transfixed, as a phantom wolf emerged out of the mist and then disappeared as quickly as it had appeared. Tala heard the song of the wolf and knew this was his spirit animal.

I saw a wolf
After a misty night
High on a ridge
Bathed in light
A phantom wolf
Ready for flight
My quest was done
My spirit in sight

Almost in a trance, Tala stumbled down the cliff.

At the bottom of the mountain was a cave which he entered as so many of his ancestors had before him. He walked down a short tunnel and came upon a small enclosure. Overcome by a strong urge to sing, Tala sang his song in a clear voice as if he had sung it hundreds of times before.

At the far end of the tunnel Tala could sense something looming in the darkness. A huge wolf materialized out of the shadows. It padded slowly toward Tala. Tala stood still, singing softly as the last trace of his boyhood disappeared and the spirit wolf merged with his body. He had shown his fearlessness during the trials and temptations of the night before. He had triumphed.

Kaya and Y searched the mountainside for Tala, until they found the cliff where he had spent the night. Kaya sensed that her twin was close by and called out. Tala heard her cry and came running to embrace his sister. Tala told Kaya and Y about the island where he knew the box had been taken. They talked until evening came, making plans to invade the island unseen. They must go at night, but even so the moon was full and might illuminate them.

Y said, "There is another way, but it is filled with dangerous creatures who are known to lurk in the depths of the ocean." They decided it was a risk they would have to take if they were to rescue their people.

Y told them how he had visited the island years ago. He described the lake at the peak of the mountain. The elders had told him that the lake was bottomless and reached down into the abyss, the deepest part of the ocean. The lake water was salt water because a cave in the ocean floor led from the abyss to the lake. The fish said to inhabit the ocean strait between the shore and the island were ferocious.

Y said, "There is perpetual darkness in the depths and the fish float along, motionless, waiting for the unwary." Y told them of the voracious Barracuda and its large mouth filled with dagger-like teeth.

Y leapt towards the twins saying, "All you might see is a flash of blue before they get you." The twins both jumped. They had been so intent on listening to Y that they were startled by his sudden movement.

Y, enjoying the limelight, continued to tell them of the Ratfish who found his victims by smell. Y sniffed loudly. He told them how the Ratfish was poisonous to touch. Then he pulled his arms into his sleeves saying, "Ratfish have retractable clasping organs that pop out and cut your skin." Y thrust his cupped hands out of his sleeves demonstrating. "The Ratfish turns many colours, but it's the eyes you'll never forget. The reflection of emerald green eyes in the dark. Almost as if the sea were alive with them."

Y grabbed a stick and hung it under his chin,

telling the twins of the Shining Loose Jaw who had extremely large teeth in its lower jaw and a large barbel, a long sensory line, which hung down beneath it. Y held a long stick under his chin swishing it back and forth, to imitate the movements of the fish. Y explained that it had a bulb on a long filament line that was luminous, and two other large organs on its head which also glowed.

"You must not exaggerate so," Tala said.

"It is true, and if it's untrue may God strike me dead," Y replied, rolling his eyes upward and then taking a quick step sideways. "All the fish I have told you of live off our coast in the deep waters. There are even more unusual fish than those I have mentioned. Fish like the Barreleye, with a flat snout and a large wedge-like head. In front of its eyes, the skin is transparent so you are able to look right into its brain. The pupils of its eyes are on top of its head," Y put his fist on top of his head, "making it truly hideous."

Kaya laughed saying, "Y, you must be making this up!"

Y said, " Laugh if you will but we'll see for ourselves shortly," indignant that the twins were so skeptical.

The twins laughed at Y's stories but their stomachs knotted in fear as they went off to sleep and dreamt of the dangers that awaited.

7

The next morning, all three stood on the shore ready to dive into the water when Y stopped Kaya and Tala saying, "Wait, I must find two special shells to help you breathe under the water." Y looked up and down the beach for a particular type of shell his father had shown him. When he finally found it he told the twins they must use it sparingly. They went to the edge of the water and plunged in, swimming out farther and farther.

They swam until the beach was only a thin, dark line. They decided to look for an entrance to the underwater cave. Tala dove first, searching, and then surfacing to report to Kaya and Y. Kaya volunteered next. She couldn't find any opening and was about to return to the surface when she saw an octopus swim into some seaweed and disappear. The seaweed swayed back and forth but there was no sign of the octopus. She swam to the surface and took a deep breath of the sweet air.

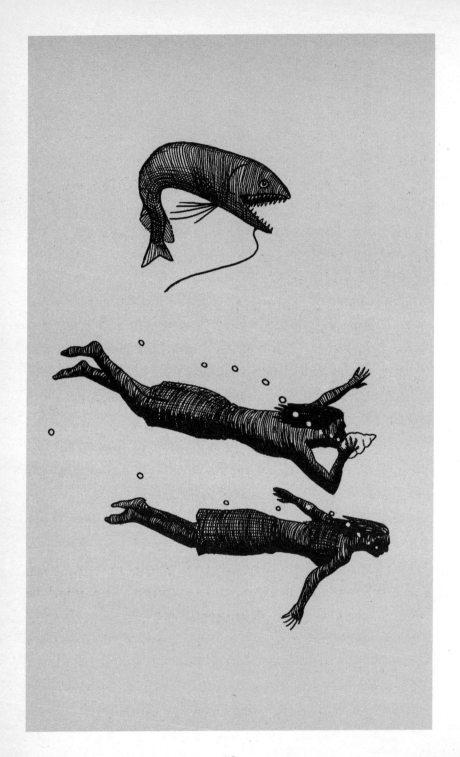

"Did you find anything?" Tala asked.

"I think an octopus has shown us the entrance," Kaya replied.

They took a deep breath and dove under. Tala parted the seaweed and revealed an opening large enough for them to swim through. They swam into a tunnel that narrowed and led upward. Their heads broke the surface and they found themselves in a small cave. Kaya pulled herself up on the ledge with Tala close behind her. Y came up spluttering and muttering to himself.

They looked around, and on the other side of the cave was another pool of water, darker and colder than the one they had just left.

"Maybe I should go ahead and report back," Y volunteered, but the twins decided they would stick together and in they plunged. It was dark and they could barely see. They needed to use the shell to breathe but remembered to conserve their air. Tala grabbed Kaya's arm. A Dragonfish swam by, its organs flickering and glowing in the dark. Its lower jaw protruded, full of large sharp teeth.

They swam quickly in the opposite direction. Kaya felt as if her lungs would burst. She tried to take a quick breath of air from her shell. It slipped out of her hand and fell to the floor. Tala and Kaya swam down to retrieve it, but just as they were about to swim upwards, a light appeared to their left.

A Viper fish was grotesquely illuminated by the

wire bobel that hung suspended from the top of its head. The gelatinous slime that covered it made it even more detestable than the other fish. Its fangs were terrifying.

Y tapped both of them on the shoulder and beckoned them to follow him into an opening which led upward to the surface. Tala and Kaya gasped for air. They were in the middle of a lake. The end of their search was close at hand. They swam toward the shore and found a rock outcropping on which to rest.

8

Night was fast approaching. They must think quickly and forge a plan to find the box. "Early in the morning, just before daybreak, we will scout out their camp," Tala said.

"If we skirt the base of the cliff and climb to the ridge, we will be better able to see the camp without being spotted," Kaya replied. "And we must have an escape route. Once the theft is discovered they will be after us like a swarm of bees."

"It will take too long to swim back," Y said.

"Perhaps Y could return with the eagle," Kaya suggested.

"Oh, sure. Y do this, Y do that, why do I have to do everything? I go and get the eagle and you two have all the adventure. It is just so unfair!" Y grumbled.

"There will be plenty of adventure for all of us, Y, and besides you will be rescuing both the box, and Kaya and me," Tala said.

"Well, when you put it that way . . . ." Y said grinning.

Their plans set, they drifted off to sleep. Moments later, a high-pitched scream ripped through the dark night. Kaya and Tala bolted upright. Y jerked the blanket up over his head.

"What is that noise?" Kaya said shakily.

Tala replied, "It is only a cougar, high up in the mountains."

Y peeked out from under his blanket and said in a squeaky little voice, "Yeah, it's only a cougar nothing to be afraid, afraid of." They finally fell into a deep sleep, exhausted from their long trip.

They awoke just before dawn. Kaya and Tala said goodbye to Y and started hiking towards the cliffs. Tala heard a sound like the beating of wings, and pointed in its direction. Kaya made a motion to Tala to move forward. They crept closer and squatted down to peek through.

On the other side, a small gully dropped into a larger ditch. There, four strange winged beings, twice as tall as a grown man, hopped around and flapped their wings. Each had the body of a man, but the head, wings and claws of a hawk. They hopped around on their haunches making sharp clicking sounds with their beaks.

They were fighting over the remains of a kill, and bones and meat scraps were scattered all over the ground. One of the hawkmen had a huge chunk of meat in his beak. Suddenly he raised his head, hearing a rustling noise in the bushes.

Tala saw him scanning the bushes and motioned to Kaya to run. The hawkman, distracted from his eating by Kaya and Tala's movement, was an easy target for the others and they ripped the choice piece of meat out of his beak.

Kaya and Tala ran towards the cliffs as quickly as two deer. The hawkmen continued to squabble and fight among themselves and the rustling sound was soon forgotten. Kaya and Tala, not daring to look back, ran breathlessly through the woods. Kaya tripped on a tree root and fell with a loud thump.

Tala stopped to help her up. "Run Tala, save yourself!" Kaya screamed.

Tala looked behind Kaya, but saw they were not being pursued. They headed through the forest to a secluded stand of trees where they saw canoes raised slightly off the ground on posts and a few elaborately carved grave boxes.

"What is this place?" Kaya asked fearfully.

"It is a sacred burial ground," Tala replied moving toward the canoe to investigate. He peered in and discovered scraps of weathered material and bones scattered on the bottom. Tools lay alongside the skeletal remains.

A D-adze carving tool and a bow and arrow lay alongside the spear. The bow and arrow had long ago disintegrated, but the spear was still intact. Tala grabbed it.

"You must not rob the dead," Kaya gasped.

"This warrior has no further need for it and we lack weapons," Tala retorted sharply, knowing full well that he was wrong to touch the spear.

"Tala, we must keep moving. The camp will be wide awake by now, " Kaya said urgently.

"Let's stay in the shadows so we are not detected," Tala replied. When they arrived at the base of the cliff, they climbed silently to the top and crawled on their stomachs toward the edge. They peered over cautiously. Directly below them was a stand of trees and at the far side of the valley the evil ones' soldiers had set up camp. They counted over a hundred tents — more than they had anticipated. "We will approach just after dusk when they cannot see us," said Kaya.

"Once they are sleeping we will make our move," Tala said.

They watched the soldiers move around the camp, trying to guess where the box was hidden. They lay on the hard ground, standing watch and waiting for their chance to sneak into camp.

As the sun started to set, the twins scrambled down the walls of the cliff. They had just reached the bottom when a shadow loomed over them. They heard a sharp clicking sound and the flap of powerful wings. The sky continued to darken as flock after flock of hawkmen returned to their cliffs to roost for the night. The evil ones kept the hawkmen for hunting and to help guard their encampment.

The twins moved liked ghosts deeper and deeper into the forest. The only sound was the rapid beating of their hearts. They walked on and on through the forest. The cold, damp air chilled them but they knew that they dare not light a fire. They found a large old tree and climbed up into it to spend the night.

"Better try and sleep, Kaya. We will need all our strength and wits about us later," said Tala.

"We are not alone, Tala, I can feel Grandfather. His spirit is here with us," Kaya said reassuringly. Tala and Kaya dozed into the long night.

When they awoke, they climbed out of the tree to stretch their stiff muscles.

Kaya and Tala cautiously set off towards the village. The dark helped cloak their movements as they crept along. Tala stopped abrubtly. Kaya bumped into him and gasped. Tala pointed to a guard sleeping outside one of the tents, his spear carelessly laying over his lap. The guard slept on, but were there others?

The twins moved, silent as ghosts. An owl hooted. Tala motioned to Kaya to enter the tent quickly. Cautiously she ducked through the door while Tala stood guard outside.

Her eyes adjusted slowly to the half-lit tent, as she tried to quickly scan the dark interior. She caught sight of the box, and moved towards it. In her haste she almost awakened a sleeping soldier lying in the middle of the floor. Kala held her breath and tiptoed closer and closer to the box. She was just about to grab it when the soldier snored loudly, rolling over. Kaya, startled, bumped the box and knocked it off the stand sending it flying into the air.

Kaya made a desperate lunge and caught the box

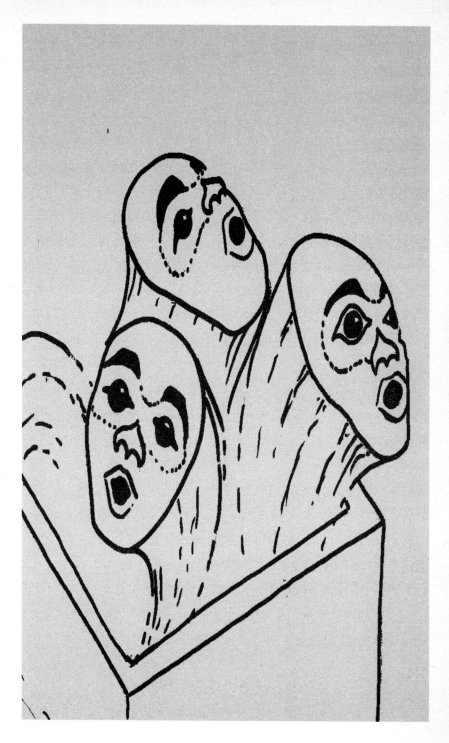

51

in mid-air before it woke the guard. She held it tightly to her body and ran out of the tent. She tripped on a tree root and almost fell but regained her balance just in time. Grasping the box even more tightly, she ran up the slope with Tala right behind her. The twins fled into the forest to hide and wait for Y. The remaining hours stretched ahead of them interminably.

10

Long before daybreak Y woke, ate breakfast and fed his eagle. He climbed on the eagle's back and went off to find Kaya and Tala, humming to himself as he flew along. Meanwhile, the hawkmen, sensing something alien in the air, set off in search of the invader.

Kaya and Tala heard their wings beating and looked up. "Oh no! Y will be killed," Kaya gasped. The hawkmen charged Y and his eagle, their talons ready to strike.

The eagle turned and twisted, barely missing the hawkmens' claws. One of the larger hawkmen knocked the eagle to one side. She let out a loud scream as the talons scraped her body. Y lost his balance with the sudden turn and plummeted through the trees, crashing to the forest floor.

"No!" Tala screamed and raced toward the spot where Y had fallen.

"Home," Y shouted. He gave this command to his faithful eagle, knowing that she would not desert him. The eagle veered sharply towards home and soon outdistanced her pursuers.

Luckily, Y's fall had been cushioned by the trees. He was badly bruised but unhurt. Tala and Kaya raced to him. He sat on the forest floor, indignantly picking twigs and leaves off his clothes.

"Come and rescue us Y, fall to the ground Y, sure, sure," he muttered to himself. Tala grabbed Y and hugged him.

"Cut it out, cut it out, none of that mushy stuff," Y said indignantly. The twins' noisy welcome woke the camp. The guard who had been sleeping in the tent discovered the theft of the box and rang an alarm bell. The soldiers grabbed their spears and raced in the direction of the commotion.

"Which way should we go?" Tala yelled.

"Don't expect me to rescue you anymore," Y said huffily.

"Quick, run into the forest," Kaya yelled. She grabbed the box and Tala reached down and yanked Y to his feet. "Run little friend, run!"

They ran into a small clearing, the soldiers voices getting louder and louder as they closed the gap between them. Tala pointed toward a wolf on a hill. Perhaps this was a sign. Tala's spirit animal would protect them and besides, they had no time to consider alternatives. They would have to trust it. The wolf waited and then turned to see if they were following. Around a small hill, they saw the wolf disappear into a cave and raced after him. The tunnel was almost pitch black and they could barely see the silvery glint of the wolf's fur as it led them deeper and deeper into the dark. They held hands so they would not become separated.

They heard a shout and voices behind them. Tala, Kaya and Y raced as fast as they could, plunging into the dark helter-skelter, to out-distance their pursuers. They came to the end of the tunnel into a large room. In front of them was a pool of black murky water too wide to cross. They would be captured and killed.

"Faster, don't let them escape!" A soilder yelled. They heard another sound, a steady chant, and paddles beating in rhythm. A Spirit Canoe appeared in front of them.

"Come quickly," the paddlers yelled.

Kaya ran toward the canoe.

Tala cautioned, "Wait, they might be trying to trick us."

They heard footsteps coming down the tunnel. They had no time to hesitate. Kaya, Tala and Y leapt into the canoe as it moved first up into the air and then down straight toward the earth. Y let out a loud gasp and shut his eyes. As the bow of the canoe met the ground, the earth parted, letting the canoe enter. A long dark tunnel led them further and further into the underworld.

Kaya held onto the box. Spirits floated toward the canoe, their shapes changing and twisting. An enormous beast with its teeth barred flew straight toward them. Y let out a scream and dropped flat in the bottom of the canoe. Kaya let out a little cry and Tala grabbed her hand. He whispered, "Remember the words of Grandfather. Keep your mind and heart pure and think only good thoughts. Close your eyes, Kaya."

Tala kept his eyes open, wondering if they were trapped. Evil spirts rushed the canoe from all sides. Y shifted up on to his knees, peeking over the sides in time to avoid a small winged snake hissing violently. Y let out a loud yelp and fell into a dead faint.

There were other spirits as well, good spirits. Tala spotted his wolf spirit for the fourth time.

> *I saw a wolf,*
> *After a misty night*
> *High on a ridge*
> *Bathed in light*
> *A phantom wolf*
> *Ready for flight*
> *Our quest is done*
> *Lead us to the light.*

The drummer in the back of the canoe and the paddlers beat in a steady rhythm. Tala's wolf ran ahead of the Spirit Canoe, leading them out of the underworld and into the bay near their village. Y, having recovered, leapt out of the canoe, and raced up the beach, anxious to tell anyone that would listen his tales of adventure and daring. Y grinned to himself as he strutted up to the villagers.

Grandfather stood in the doorway of his house. Kaya ran and knelt before him, extending the box.

"You have proven yourselves and served our people well," Grandfather said opening the box. The spirits of the people returned to the village. The nation was once more whole.

A great feast was planned to celebrate. Kaya, Tala and Y took places of honour in the bighouse. As this quest came to an end, the twins were already imagining others and the adventures they would be guided through by the fearless wolf who waited for them high on a mountain top to the north.